GROSSET & DUNLAP
Published by the Penguin Group
Penguin Group (USA) Inc., 375 Hudson Street,
New York, New York 10014, USA
Penguin Group (Canada), 90 Eglinton Avenue East,
Suite 700, Toronto, Ontario M4P 2Y3, Canada
(a division of Pearson Penguin Canada Inc.)
Penguin Books Ltd., 80 Strand, London WC2R 0RL, England
Penguin Group Ireland, 25 St. Stephen's Green, Dublin 2, Ireland
(a division of Penguin Books Ltd.)
Penguin Group (Australia), 250 Camberwell Road,
Camberwell, Victoria 3124, Australia
(a division of Pearson Australia Group Pty. Ltd.)
Penguin Books India Pvt. Ltd., 11 Community Centre,
Panchsheel Park, New Delhi—110 017, India
Penguin Group (NZ), 67 Apollo Drive, Rosedale,
North Shore 0632, New Zealand
(a division of Pearson New Zealand Ltd.)
Penguin Books (South Africa) (Pty.) Ltd., 24 Sturdee Avenue,
Rosebank, Johannesburg 2196, South Africa

Penguin Books Ltd., Registered Offices:
80 Strand, London WC2R 0RL, England

www.speedracer.com

Designed by Michelle Martinez Design, Inc.

Library of Congress Cataloging-in-Publication Data is available.

ISBN 978-0-448-44808-4   10 9 8 7 6 5 4 3 2 1

SPEED RACER™

The Most
Dangerous Race

by Chase Wheeler   Grosset & Dunlap

The Marvels of the Mach 5

The Mach 5 is one of the most
powerful and amazing racing cars in
the world. Pops Racer designed the Mach 5
with features you won't see on any other car.
All of the features can be controlled by
buttons on the steering wheel.

A This button releases powerful jacks to boost the car so Sparky, the mechanic, can quickly make any necessary repairs or adjustments.

B Press this button and the Mach 5 sprouts special grip tires for traction over any terrain. At the same time, an incredible 5,000 torque of horsepower is distributed equally to each wheel by auxiliary engines.

C For use when Speed Racer has to race over heavily wooded terrain, powerful rotary saws protrude from the front of the Mach 5 to slash and cut any and all obstacles.

D Pressing the D button releases a powerful deflector that seals the cockpit into an air-conditioned, crash and bulletproof, watertight chamber. Inside it, Speed Racer is completely isolated and shielded.

E The button for special illumination allows Speed Racer to see much farther and more clearly than with ordinary headlights. It's invaluable in some of the weird and dangerous places he races the Mach 5.

F Press this button when the Mach 5 is underwater. First the cockpit is supplied with oxygen, then a periscope is raised to scan the surface of the water. Everything that is seen is relayed down to the cockpit by television.

G This releases a homing robot from the front of the car. The homing robot can carry pictures or tape-recorded messages to anyone or anywhere Speed Racer wants.

"Ladies and gentlemen!" the announcer called. "The fabulous Stunt Car Spectacular is about to begin."

The crowd cheered. They could not wait to see the wild tricks the cars would perform.

The announcer tipped her top hat to the crowd. She spun around, her skirt twirling in the air. "Get ready for action and thrills!" she said. "There will be rewards for the most skillful and daring drivers."

The show was open to any driver who dared to compete. Everyone knew the dangers involved, but there were some who were willing to take the risk. The first event was to jump over seven race cars that were piled on top of one another.

"The first contestant is Mr. Guts Wheeler," the announcer said over the loudspeaker.

Guts waved to the crowd from inside his car. He was wearing a red racing helmet and was driving a silver car.

Guts floored the gas pedal and sped up a ramp toward the tower of cars. He drove faster and faster, trying to pick up speed. But when he reached the top of the ramp . . . *CRASH!* Guts's car smacked right into the tower. He didn't make it! The crowd groaned.

"The next contestant is Mr. Hy Octane," the announcer said.

The crowd held their breath as Hy Octane revved his engine and sped up the ramp. Up, up he flew, heading for the top of the pile of cars. *Crash!* His car hit the car at the top of tower and burst into flames! Hy Octane was hurt, but he was able to walk away from the crash.

People were beginning to grow restless. Would anyone be able to make it over the tower today?

Just then, a girl in the crowd spotted someone. "Isn't that Speed Racer?" she asked her friend.

Speed Racer was the most famous race car driver in the world.

"That's him, all right," the other girl said. They ran off to meet the superstar.

"Hi, can we have your autograph?" one of the girls asked Speed.

"Boy, oh, boy. Isn't my brother Speed popular?" Speed's little brother Sprite said.

"And cute, too," the other girl added, blushing.

Speed smiled and gave the girls autographs.

"Thanks, Speed," the girls said.

Speed's girlfriend, Trixie, moved closer to Speed

and smiled. The girls, happy that they had gotten Speed's autograph, walked away. Trixie sighed. She knew that Speed had a lot of fans, but it was hard to get used to all the attention he got.

"So, you must be Speed Racer," a man said, walking up to Speed.

"Huh?" Speed said, caught off guard. This man didn't look like a fan. He was wearing a red-and-yellow striped helmet with a dark visor over his eyes. Who was he?

"I was told you were one of the greatest racers in the world," the man said. "Is that true?"

"Who are you?" Speed wanted to know.

"Snake Oiler's the name, and I'm afraid I'm a pretty good racer myself. Why don't we have a race sometime to see which one of us is better?" he said as he jumped into his car.

Speed loved to race. And he could never give up a challenge. "You're on!" Speed said, with a determined look on his face.

"Make the pile of cars higher!" Snake shouted

to the mechanic.

The crowd gasped. No one had been able to make it over the tower of cars as it was. How could someone make it over if it was even higher?

"You'll never be able to make it!" the mechanic told Snake.

Snake looked angry. "Don't argue with me. Just make it higher."

The mechanic did as Snake wanted, and used a crane to add more cars to the pile.

"Next is Snake Oiler," the announcer said.

Snake sped up the ramp and flipped over the tower of cars, his car somersaulting in the air. And

amazingly, his car landed on the other side of the pile, right side up!

The crowd roared as Snake sped away to safety.

"He did it!" the announcer shouted. "Snake Oiler just drove over the biggest stack we've had yet. Mr. Oiler is the star member of the world famous Car Acrobatic Team."

He's on the Car Acrobatic Team, huh? Speed thought. *Well, I've sure heard of them.*

"All right, ladies and gentlemen. Who'll try and beat him?" the announcer asked.

Snake Oiler got out of his car and walked over to Speed. "I was just warming up. Everyone's going to have to do some fancy driving to beat that. How about you, Speed? Can you beat me?"

"I don't know," Speed admitted, brushing back his brown hair with his hand.

Upon hearing Speed's answer, Spritle became upset. He couldn't believe that his brother doubted himself. "What do you mean, Speed?" he asked, huffing and puffing. "You can beat him!"

He ran up to his brother and pounded him on his chest. "Go ahead, try it," Sprittle pleaded. "Are you scared?"

"You better not try it," Snake Oiler said, stepping up to the brothers. "Because if you crash, I'll lose my best competitor in the Alpine Race."

The Alpine Race was the most dangerous race in the world. It was also a race that Speed Racer wanted to compete in.

Speed thought for a moment. He wanted to drive in the Alpine Race, but he also did not want to turn down Snake's challenge here. He was not a quitter—he was Speed Racer, the best race car driver in the world! "I'll try," Speed said, running to his car.

Sprittle and his pet chimpanzee, Chim Chim, jumped up and down with joy. Speed was going to try to jump over the tower of cars!

Speed got into his sleek white car. This was the Mach 5 and his dad, Pops Racer, had designed it. The Mach 5 was the ultimate racing machine. The car could accelerate in the blink of an eye, and could handle every twist and turn on the road. In the Mach 5, Speed felt like he could take on anything—even the challenge of flying over a tower of cars!

"I'll get to the top!" Speed said, starting the engine.

Just as Speed started the engine, Trixie and Sparky, Speed's best friend and mechanic, came running up. "Don't, Speed. You'll never make it," Trixie said, putting her arms around him.

Speed looked up at Trixie. She was very smart, and Speed knew that she'd only warn him if she

really thought he was in danger.

"Trixie's right," Sparky agreed. "Don't do it."

Speed looked around. The crowd was growing restless. They wanted Speed to try the trick. But his friends were right—it was too dangerous.

"Remember how important the big Alpine Race will be," Trixie said. "If something happens, you'll be out of it. Just look how high that stack is."

Speed thought for a moment. *She's right*, he thought. *If I'm gonna beat Snake, then I'll beat him in the Alpine Race. I'll have a better chance to win that. I've got to. I've got to win the Alpine Race!*

Spritle saw his brother hesitating, and he was not happy. "I know Speed can drive over that," he said to Trixie. "But right now he's nothing but a scared chicken."

"He is brave," Trixie told Spritle. "It takes real courage not to challenge Snake here, but to wait for the Alpine Race."

Spritle scratched his chin. "Hmmm. Seems complicated."

"You'll understand when it comes time for the race," Trixie told him.

"I hope so," Spritle said with a shrug.

Just then, Speed heard a hum of car engines. He turned and looked at the horizon. The crowd gasped. They could not believe their eyes. A group of nine race cars was heading toward them. As Speed watched, the cars flew into the air and neatly landed one on top of one another—all while continuing to drive! All the cars were black, except for the bottom one, which was red.

"It's the Car Acrobatic Team!" Trixie shouted.

"Daredevil drivers!" Speed added.

The top cars shot off from the bottom red car one by one and headed straight toward Trixie and Speed! Just before they were about to crash into them, the cars flew over Trixie and Speed. The crowd screamed. The cars whirled above Speed and his friends' heads. As the cars sped around faster and faster, Speed and his friends got dizzier and dizzier until they were knocked to the ground.

Speed was dazed but not hurt. He stood up, wiping the dust from his pants.

"We'll be seeing you in the Alpine Race," Snake Oiler shouted from one of the cars.

And with that, the Car Acrobatic Team drove off into the distance.

Speed wanted more than anything to enter the Alpine Race—and win. So he and his friends traveled to the Alps, where the race would take place.

"Well, Speed, here we are," Sparky said, pointing to the snowcapped mountains in the distance. "But I don't think you should enter the big race. It'll be too dangerous to try."

"Why do you say that?" Speed asked as they sat down on the grass.

"Snake Oiler is one of the best drivers I've ever seen," Sparky told him. "And I think some of the other drivers on the team are even better."

Speed looked at the green flowered hills that led up to the mountains. The terrain up there sure looked dangerous, but Speed knew he was up for the challenge. "I've got to race," Speed told his friend. "I've got to beat the Car Acrobatic Team. I've got to prove that I'm the best." Speed had a very determined look on his face. "And I'm racing, no matter what you tell me."

"But they're tricky, Speed. They'll use every dirty trick to win," Sparky said, trying to get Speed to change his mind.

Speed was growing angry with his friend. "Do you think I'm afraid? Is that what you really think about me?"

Suddenly, Speed grabbed Sparky by the front of his shirt. "Cut it out!" Speed shouted at Sparky. "I'm not scared!" And with that, he shoved Sparky.

"Sparky!" Trixie yelled, coming to her friend's aid. She helped Sparky to his feet. But Sparky was done trying to talk Speed out of the race. With a sad look on his face, he walked away.

"Sparky was only trying to think about what's best for you!" Trixie said once Sparky had gone.

But Speed wouldn't listen to Trixie, either. He was going to enter the race no matter what!

Speed knew that he needed to practice if he wanted a shot at winning the race. Pops found the perfect place to practice—a track that twisted and turned in many directions. If Speed could master the tricky turns of the practice track, then he'd have no problems once he hit the Alpine course.

I'm gonna win, Speed thought as he drove the Mach 5 along the track. *I'm gonna beat Snake Oiler and everyone in the Car Acrobatic Team.*

Speed was so confident that he was sure he'd even drive better than the best racer he'd ever seen—Racer X!

"Go, Speed, go!" Spritle called from the sidelines as Speed raced past.

Pops looked at his stopwatch. "One hundred and eighty!" he shouted. Speed clocked a great time.

Speed slowed the Mach 5 to a stop. "You've done enough practicing on this course, Speed,"

Pops said. "Now it's time to practice the first jump of the Alpine course."

Speed knew that Pops was right. It was time to see if he could maneuver the Mach 5 across a deep cavern. Speed looked at the road. Huge orange and black rocks jutted out all around him. Speed would have to drive the Mach 5 around and over the rocks until the road ended. Then he would have to leap over a huge chasm and land on the other side.

"If you don't make the jump, you'll fall one thousand feet into the river," Pops warned Speed.

Speed looked down into the chasm. *Wow, it's sure a long way down!* he thought. *But I know I can make it.*

"You've got to make it!" Pops warned, as if he were reading Speed's mind.

Speed climbed into the Mach 5 and revved

the engine. But just as Pops was about to give him the start signal, Speed heard something coming up behind him.

"The Car Acrobatic Team!" Spritle shouted.

Speed couldn't believe his eyes. The Car Acrobatic Team was getting ready to leap across the chasm.

Speed watched in amazement as the team zoomed off the cliff's edge straight toward the other side. And as they flew across, the cars twirled around in the air, looking just like corkscrews!

But Speed was not intimidated. In fact, seeing this spectacular jump made him more determined

than ever to try it himself!

Speed pushed his helmet visor over his eyes and locked his seat belt.

"Good luck!" Pops shouted as Speed careened down the road at a breakneck speed. The ride looked choppy, but Pops knew that Speed was in control.

Suddenly, a yellow racing car shot up behind Speed. *Who could that be?* Speed wondered. He slammed on the gas pedal, urging the Mach 5 to go faster. But he was no match for the yellow car that was rapidly gaining on him. Soon, the yellow car boxed him in and forced him to pull over.

What Speed didn't know was that the driver of this car was really his older brother, Rex, who ran away from home many years ago. Speed only knew this driver as Racer X. It was hard to see what Racer X really looked like since he wore a black helmet that almost masked his entire face. Sleek blue goggles covered his eyes.

"What's the big idea?" Speed shouted out the window at Racer X.

"I came to warn you," Racer X told Speed. "It's too dangerous."

And as soon as Racer X said these words, rocks tumbled down the side of a nearby cliff. As the rocks fell, they picked up speed, destroying everything in their path. It was an avalanche! Speed watched in amazement as the rocks fell.

"Be careful of falling rocks like those," Racer X cautioned calmly. "Last year, they wiped out a dozen drivers who could have crossed easily."

"How could they have done that?" Speed wanted to know.

Racer X went on to tell Speed that most drivers only worried about the cars ahead of them and how to catch up and pass them. So they sometimes forgot to concentrate on the course itself.

"The plateau areas around here are very tricky," Racer X said. "The ground is hard. But when it rains heavily, the ground loosens and can cause tires to skid treacherously. Take my advice, Speed. Otherwise, this will be your last race. Very few

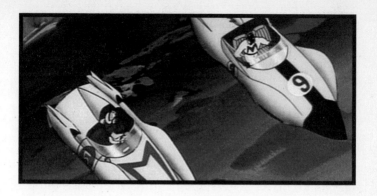

cars ever reach the finish line—it's just too dangerous."

Speed listened carefully to what Racer X told him. Racer X was an experienced driver, and Speed knew that his advice was good. But what was Racer X really saying? Was he just telling Speed to be careful, or was he warning him not to race?

"Do you think I can't win, Racer X?" Speed wanted to know.

"You can, but only if you keep your mind strictly on the hazards of the course," Racer X said.

Speed was relieved that Racer X thought he had a chance after all.

"But there's one more thing," Racer X added. "And listen carefully—as you race down toward the big jump, don't go too fast. Because if you do, you'll cause another landslide and crash down into the river."

Speed nodded.

Then Racer X told Speed that when he reached the other side and started to climb again, he shouldn't try to go up toward the top. Instead, he should zigzag along the slope. Racer X said that might take longer, but it was safer, and in the long run he would pick up some time.

"Remember, throughout the race there are patches of ice. One strong twist of your steering wheel and that will be the end of you," Racer X said. "This is the toughest course you've ever raced. You'll need every ounce of experience and skill, Speed."

"Thanks for the advice," Speed said. "I'll try to follow all of it, Racer X."

Racer X laughed and said, "Well, if you don't

run a good race, I won't enjoy winning!" He adjusted his purple driving gloves.

"You'll be in the Alpine Race?" Speed asked. He couldn't believe his ears. Why did Racer X give him all that advice if he was racing, too?

Racer X jumped into his car. "I'm going to win the Alpine Race," he told Speed with a smile. "And I'm not going to give you a break!"

Then, Racer X sped off, leaving Speed behind in his dust.

Pops Racer knew that the Mach 5 needed work. He had to improve the car in some way so Speed could win the race. But what could he do to the car? The supercharged Mach 5 was already the best car on the racing circuit. Its unique aerodynamic design and special added devices made the Mach 5 the leader of the pack. Still, the Car Acrobatic Team was a stiff competitor. Pops had seen the team perform some fantastic tricks—and the race hadn't even begun.

Pops stared at the plans he had placed on his worktable. They were good, but not good enough. Frustrated, he crumpled up the paper and tossed it in the garbage. But he wasn't about to give up. He knew he'd come up with a way to redesign the Mach 5. Then Speed would leave the Car Acrobatic Team in his dust!

That night, after dinner, Speed, Pops, and Spritle sat around the table and talked.

"The Car Acrobatic Team has some amazing drivers!" Pops said. "They're tricky, experienced, and fast. They've got some other tricks, too. But I can't figure out what they are."

"If I can find out, I might be able to beat them," Speed said.

"Right," Pops agreed. "To win, one should know the strengths and weaknesses of the competition."

Pops and Speed continued their conversation, but Spritle was bored. He had heard enough talk about the Alpine Race. As he thought about what he could do to have some fun, Chim Chim tried to swipe a cookie off his plate.

"Not so fast," Spritle told his pet chimpanzee.

But Chim Chim wanted a cookie. So when Spritle wasn't looking, he tried to steal one again.

Spritle, figuring out what Chim Chim was up to, raised his hand to knock the chimp's hand away. But when Spritle's hand came down, it landed in a can of red paint! Clever Chim Chim had pulled a fast one on Spritle! He had switched the cookie plate with the paint. The paint can flew in the air and landed right on top of Spritle's head!

But Spritle didn't have time to get angry at Chim Chim. He was listening to what Speed was saying: "Gee, Pops, it won't be so easy to find out because that team comes and goes so fast."

This gave Spritle an idea.

Later that night, when everyone was asleep,

Spritle and Chim Chim sneaked out of the house. Chim Chim followed Spritle through the woods until they came to an old beat-up car. The pair jumped in the car—their secret mission had begun!

And, of course, since this was a secret mission, they had to wear disguises. They both had on top hats. Spritle was also wearing a monocle over one eye and a cape around his shoulders.

They drove through the woods, past busy woodpeckers and hooting owls. The sky was dark, and the wind howled. A chill ran down Spritle's spine—the woods were sure creepy at night!

They came to a rope bridge that hung high over a river. Spritle steered the car over the bridge

to the other side. Suddenly, a huge bear appeared in front of the car. Baring its teeth, the creature headed straight toward them! Thinking quickly, Spritle threw the car into reverse. They sped backward over the rope bridge with the bear in pursuit. Just as they made it to the other side, the bridge snapped in two. Had the bear fallen into the river below?

No! The bear climbed up the side of the cliff and continued its chase. Down, down a snowy mountainside they sped. Oh, no! The road was about to end. A few feet farther and they would plummet off the edge of a cliff! Spritle shifted the car again, and they turned completely around, racing past the bear, which was running in the opposite direction. It finally looked as if they were safe!

As Spritle and Chim Chim continued to race away, they came to another end of a road. There was no time to turn back! Spritle knew he had two choices—either jump off the cliff to the other side, or plummet far, far below. Closing his eyes,

Spritle urged the car to fly across the chasm. *Boom!* As the car hit the ground on the other side, it exploded. Luckily, Spritle and Chim Chim were not hurt. But the car was destroyed. At least they had gotten away from that bear.

Spritle kicked a burned tire in frustration. Chim Chim was upset, too. He was jumping up and down next to the cliff's edge.

Spritle walked over to comfort his pet. But as he got closer to Chim Chim, Spritle saw that he was not upset. In fact, he seemed excited as he pointed to something below. Spritle raced over to see what Chim Chim had found.

It was the Car Acrobatic Team! All the drivers were standing at attention on the roofs of their cars, which were neatly lined up in two rows. They were carrying torches and listening to their leader, Captain Terror.

Spritle shuddered with fear as he looked at the man. He wore a long, flowing black robe, and he had goggles on his skull-like face.

It seemed as though the other racers feared Captain Terror as well. Silently, they listened to his warning: "Members of the Car Acrobatic Team," he began, "tomorrow, the great Alpine Race begins—a race which we must not lose!"

"We will not lose! We will win!" the team responded, sounding like robots.

Captain Terror seemed pleased. "Good. Now, let us gather our strength from the violence of the elements."

And with that, a cold wind whipped through the air.

"I have decided to enter seven of you in the Alpine Race," Captain Terror informed the group. "The fastest, trickiest, and most ruthless seven! Cobra will read off the names." Captain Terror handed his henchman a few sheets of paper.

As Cobra called out the names, the drivers stepped forward. "Tiger. Knuckles. Brawn. Ugly. Poison. Ender. Snake. You must observe Captain Terror's first and most important racing rule: Do anything to win, stop at nothing, and if you have to break the law . . . break it!"

Upon hearing this, Spritle was terrified. But he knew that this was his chance to help Speed. So he pulled out his camera and started snapping pictures of the team and their cars. Spritle's secret mission was a success!

Back home, Spritle showed his pictures to Pops, Speed, and Trixie. "And there's my best shot. You can see the whole bottom of the car. Chim Chim and I did a great job of spying."

"But the cars don't seem to have anything unusual on them," Trixie said, looking closely at the photos.

"Look carefully, Trixie," Pops said. "You'll see that every one of them has a special device to help them jump. You can see it's located right here." He pointed to a spot in one of the photos. "This particular part acts like a wing when the car's in the air."

Trixie nodded. She could see what Pops was talking about.

"They must have a clever designer, eh, Pops?" Speed said.

"The cleverest man in the entire racing world," Pops replied.

Sprito looked worried. "Then the Mach 5 has no chance of winning," he said.

"I'm afraid the other cars are much better than the Mach 5," Pops agreed.

Now Sprito looked angry. "Oh, please, you've

got to do something!" He pounded on Pops's arms with his fists.

Pops smiled reassuringly. "Don't worry, Spritle. I built the Mach 5, so now I'm rebuilding it."

"That's what I like to hear!" Spritle said, relieved. "Get to work!"

Pops turned to Speed. "Speed, don't forget: Driver and car have to be equally good to win, so do your best job," he said in a serious tone.

"I'll do the best job I can!" Speed said confidently.

"Hurry, Pops! Start rebuilding the Mach 5!" Spritle shouted. And with that, he and Chim Chim pushed Pops toward the car.

"I'll help, too!" Trixie said, flexing her muscles.

The group headed to the garage to get to work. Pops put on his welding gear and held a torch to the car. Speed stood at a workbench and adjusted some machinery. Each time Pops or Speed needed a part, Trixie, Spritle, and Chim Chim were ready to help out.

The work was exhausting. So exhausting, in fact, that eventually Trixie, Spritle, and Chim Chim fell asleep.

Pops looked over at the sleeping group and smiled. "You should get some rest, too, Speed. I'll finish up."

"I'm all right, Pops. You better get some rest yourself," Speed insisted.

"You have a big race tomorrow and you have to be in top condition for it!" Pops shot back. "Now don't argue with me! When I tell you to do something, you'd better do it!"

Speed knew that it was no use arguing with

Pops. After all, he was right, Speed needed his rest. And so, while everyone slept, Pops worked on the Mach 5.

In the morning, Trixie went into the garage to bring Pops some coffee. But as soon as she went inside, she saw that Pops was lying on the floor. And it didn't look like he was just sleeping—something was desperately wrong!

"Speed! Come here quickly!" Trixie shouted, dropping the coffee and rushing to Pops's side.

Hearing Trixie's voice, Speed rushed into the garage to see what had happened.

"He has a bad fever," Trixie said, feeling Pops's forehead.

"Oh, no!" Speed cried. He lifted Pops up on his back and carried him out of the garage.

"Where are you taking him, Speed?" Trixie asked.

"To the nearest hospital," Speed replied, putting Pops into the car.

"Let me take him," Trixie insisted. "You've

only got a few more hours before the race starts. You've got to finish the Mach 5."

"But Pops is more important," Speed said.

"Pops wants you to be in the race, Speed. And if he were able to, he'd tell you that himself," Trixie reasoned. "Now you get back to work on the Mach 5 while I take him to the hospital. Go ahead!"

And with that, Trixie sped off. Speed watched the car disappear and then headed back to the garage. He had a car to fix—and a race to win.

Speed knew he had to work fast. The Alpine Race was starting in a half hour, and there was still a lot to do. Speed thought about Sparky. Not only was he a good friend, but he was a great mechanic. *I only wish Sparky was here to help,* Speed thought. Then Speed remembered their argument. He knew that it was his fault that Sparky had left. But there was no time to think about that now—Speed had a race to get to.

The sun was starting to come up over the snowcapped mountains. A helicopter hovered over the starting line of the Alpine Race. Eighty-five cars were gathered there, most getting last-minute adjustments before the starting gun went off.

"Ladies and gentlemen," the announcer, who was in the helicopter, said to the crowd gathered in the stadium to watch the start of the race, "I'm flying above the Alpine Race course. As you may know, this is the most grueling race in the world. The drivers must race for three days and nights, facing all kinds of dangers. Already, more than one million spectators have gathered to witness this spectacular car classic. And we can promise them and you people watching your television sets more thrills, more chills than you have ever seen before!"

As the announcer spoke, Speed was still

working on the Mach 5. There were only twenty minutes left until the start!

"Here comes the Car Acrobatic Team," the announcer said. "Seven of the fastest and trickiest drivers anyone has ever seen anywhere."

Snake Oiler peered out of his car's window to check out the competition. "I knew Speed Racer would be too yellow to turn up!"

"And driving car number nine," the announcer continued, "is the mysterious Racer X. Nobody knows who he is or where he comes from."

"All entries, take your starting position!" the

announcer called. "It's fifteen minutes until race time."

Back at the garage, Speed was lowering the chassis down onto the Mach 5's body frame. Now he only had a few final adjustments to make. "I'll see if the wings work," Speed said, pressing a button.

"They do!" he exclaimed as a pair of white wings shot out from under the car doors.

Now Speed knew he had a chance of winning the race. Wiping the sweat from his face, he hopped into the Mach 5, snapped on his helmet, and revved the engine. He had three minutes to make it to the starting line.

As Speed entered the stadium, the countdown had already begun. Five, four, three, two . . . Speed made it just in time!

"Here comes a last-minute entry. It's the Mach 5 driven by Speed Racer!" the announcer shouted as Speed zoomed to the starting line.

In a flash, the cars took off, speeding furiously

down the track. The crowd roared, cheering on their favorite drivers.

From behind a column, a lone fan stepped out—it was Sparky! But he was not cheering with the rest of the crowd. In fact, he had a worried look on his face.

"Try to win, Speed," Sparky whispered as the cars left the stadium. "But most of all—be careful!"

The cars noisily whizzed through the opening stretch of the Alpine Race, against a backdrop of snowcapped mountains. Speed gripped the Mach 5's steering wheel, urging the car to stay on course and go faster. Dangerous curves hugged the sides of the hills, and Speed witnessed many cars spinning out of control, bursting through the guardrails, and ending in fiery crashes. Speed had to use all the concentration he could muster to stay on the course.

Although Speed was a fierce competitor, he knew that the tricky Car Acrobatic Team was favored to win the race. But what the Car Acrobatic Team didn't know was that Speed was driving a car designed with wings, too. As Speed drove, he felt grateful that Pops had redesigned the Mach 5. Now he had a chance to win!

Yet Speed wasn't completely happy. He was still worried about Pops. "I'm glad Trixie got him to the hospital, and I hope he's all right," Speed said to himself.

The cars climbed higher and higher into the Alps. Out of the corner of his eye, Speed spied huge icicles dangling from the cliffs' edges. He shuddered to think about what would happen if one of those icicles were to come loose and fall! He gripped the steering wheel harder and pressed on.

Just then, a tight curve sprung up from out of nowhere. Speed pumped the brakes a bit, but something was wrong. The brakes didn't feel right.

Luckily, Speed cleared the curve. But, he couldn't understand what could be wrong with his brakes. After all, both he and Pops had given the Mach 5 a thorough once-over.

As Speed raced on, he saw the first checkpoint up ahead. Two men in light blue jumpsuits and caps ran out to meet him. Speed handed one of the men a document.

"The Mach 5 driven by Speed Racer, heh?" one of the men said after reading the paper. "Well, you're running ninth. You better hurry up!"

So Speed wasn't in such a great position after all. "I'll try," Speed told the man.

"There'll be bad weather ahead, so take extra precaution," the man warned as he serviced the Mach 5.

"Thanks for the advice," Speed said as he headed back to the road.

The Mach 5 sped down the road, leaving a cloud of dust in its wake. Up ahead, the snow-capped mountains rose from the horizon. As the Mach 5 hugged the edge of the road, Speed once again felt that there was something wrong with the brakes.

He touched the brake pedal again as the Mach 5 wound around the curves. "I thought I had adjusted the brakes correctly, but Sparky's the expert on things like that. If only he'd been there to do it. I shouldn't have argued with him."

Speed knew his friend had only warned him not to enter the race because he was worried about him. Sparky was a good friend, and Speed shouldn't have gotten so angry with him.

"I wish Sparky hadn't left," Speed said with a sigh.

⚙   ⚙   ⚙   ⚙

Deep in the woods, a tan convertible sedan cruised at top speed. The passengers were Spritle and Chim Chim, and the driver was—Sparky! Even though he had argued with Speed, Sparky couldn't stay angry long. Plus, he had a feeling that Speed needed him.

"I hope Speed's all right," Sparky said to Spritle. "I know those brakes on the Mach 5 won't last. They have to be changed before the first hour of the race is up. It's important."

Upon hearing this, Spritle was upset. "If you hadn't argued with him you would have been there to fix Speed's brakes!" Spritle said.

Chim Chim jumped up and down in agreement.

Yet Sparky wasn't about to get angry at Spritle for what he said. He knew that Spritle was just worried about his older brother.

But before Sparky had a chance to say anything to Spritle, the car's engine began to rattle. Then it sputtered and coughed. Finally, it died. Sparky got out of the car and popped the hood.

"Hurry, Sparky!" Spritle called. "You've got to get this car moving. We have to find Speed and fix the Mach 5's brakes."

But all Sparky could do was shake his head. The car was dead. And not even Sparky, who was a mechanical genius, could fix it. They were doomed. And if they couldn't reach Speed in time, he would be, too!

Trixie looked out the window of Pops's hospital room. It was a beautiful day. The sky was blue, the sun was shining, and the birds were chirping in the trees. Usually, a day like this would make Trixie feel happy. But today she was worried. She was sad that Pops was sick and in the hospital. And she was worried about Speed driving in the Alpine Race. She had a feeling that something had gone wrong and that Speed needed her help.

She turned around to face Pops. He was lying in the hospital bed with a white sheet drawn up to his neck. At his side were a nurse and Mom Racer.

"Oh, I hope Sparky's been able to reach Speed with the new brakes," Trixie said.

"It is my fault that Speed entered the race with faulty brakes . . . my fault . . . my fault," Pops sputtered in pain.

"Pops," Mom Racer said, "the doctor said you mustn't get excited."

Trixie knew that Mom Racer was right. It was best not to worry Pops. Trixie shook her head. *There's no use sitting around here worrying,* she thought. *I've got to do something!*

Trixie's eyes brightened. "I'll try to catch up to Speed by helicopter. I've got to see him," she said.

But Mom Racer looked concerned. "A helicopter might crash. They're expecting a storm up there," she cautioned.

"Maybe I can get there before the storm hits," Trixie said with a determined look on her face.

And with that, she raced out of the room.

⚫ ⚫ ⚫ ⚫

Once inside her helicopter, Trixie headed for the Alpine Race course. She flew above the snowcapped mountains looking for the Mach 5. Suddenly, she spotted Spritle, Sparky, Chim Chim,

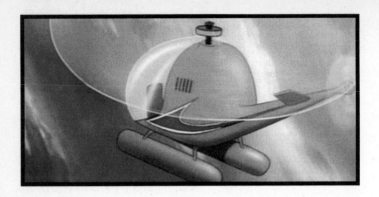

and their broken-down car.

"I better go pick them up," Trixie said out loud.

Down below, Sparky, Spritle, and Chim Chim heard a helicopter whirring above their heads.

"Look, it's Trixie!" Spritle shouted, pointing toward the sky.

Trixie positioned the helicopter over the car and let down a rope ladder.

Sparky reached up and grabbed on to the ladder. As he swung from the swaying rope, he looked down to find Spritle and Chim Chim. But they hadn't moved! They were sitting with their legs crossed and arms folded on the hood of the car.

"Come on, Spritle!" Sparky shouted.

"I'm a big boy—I don't need help from a girl!" Spritle said with a frown.

"Come up here, Spritle," Trixie said impatiently. "We've got to help Speed and we have very little time!"

"Come on, Spritle!" Sparky urged. He was still swinging from the rope ladder and did not know how much longer he could hold on.

"Go without us!" Spritle said stubbornly.

Sparky shrugged. "Suit yourself, then!"

Spritle watched the helicopter as it climbed back up into the sky, carrying Sparky by the ladder.

"Wait for me!" Spritle cried out suddenly, changing his mind.

As he and Chim Chim dashed for the rope, they slipped off the side of the mountain!

They began to plummet down, their arms and legs flapping furiously. "I changed my mind!" Spritle shouted.

Trixie flew into action and lowered the helicopter. In an instant, the rope ladder flew in

front of Spritle's face. Thinking quickly, he caught the ladder with his teeth, and Chim Chim's teeth caught the bottom of Spritle's pants' leg. The two swung back and forth on the ladder as the helicopter sped away into the distance.

The Alpine Race continued as the drivers sped down a mountain road. From the Mach 5, Speed could see Snake Oiler and the other members of the Car Acrobatic Team up ahead.

Speed raced through a dark tunnel and turned

on his headlights. "Now's my chance to pull ahead," he said, flooring the engine. The Mach 5 flew over the icy road, past six cars.

Racer X, who was driving behind Speed, became alarmed as he watched Speed drive. "What's Speed doing?" he asked himself. "We're over ice now and he's liable to go into a bad skid."

Despite the dangerous conditions of the tunnel's road, Speed pressed on. He was determined to gain the lead. As he passed Snake Oiler and the rest of the Car Acrobatic Team, Speed smiled.

But the Car Acrobatic Team had a tricky plan up their sleeves. "Now we'll give Speed a little surprise!" Snake Oiler said, pressing a button on his dashboard. Snake's red signal light began to flash and beep. Seeing Snake's signal, the other Car Acrobatic drivers turned on their car wings. At once, the team took to the air and soared over the Mach 5. As they flew, they knocked the sharp icicles down from the tunnel's ceiling.

"Ugh!" Speed cried as the broken ice pelted the Mach 5.

Racer X, who was trailing Speed, was hit by the flying ice, too.

Quickly, Speed swerved to avoid being hit by the ice. But the road was slippery, and the Mach 5 was losing traction. Speed couldn't hold on, and the Mach 5 began to spin out of control! Many of the other cars were having a hard time, too, and crashed into walls and other cars.

Concentrating hard, Speed guided the Mach 5 out of the path of the flying ice and crashing cars. He flew out of the tunnel, onto the open road.

"Whoa!" Speed shouted as he tried to press the brake pedal. But nothing happened. The brakes wouldn't work at all!

The Mach 5 rounded an icy curve, still out of control. Thinking fast, Speed tugged at the emergency brake as he struggled to control the steering wheel. As the car slowed down, it rolled closer and closer to the edge of the road with a deep dropoff. The Mach 5's rear wheels spun, desperately trying to gain some traction. But it was no use—the Mach 5 was barely hanging on to the sharp angle of the mountainside.

Speed's heart was pounding, and his hands were sweating. The car teetered dangerously on the mountainside. If he moved one more inch backward, he'd be history! Suddenly, a huge cluster of boulders began to slide down the mountainside. The earth beneath the Mach 5 trembled, and the car shook. Before Speed knew it, the car was careening down the mountainside backward.

And all Speed could do was scream.

"Calling Speed! Calling Speed!" Sparky shouted into the helicopter's radio. "What's your present location?"

There was no answer.

Sprite was worried about his brother. *Where can he be?* he wondered.

Just then, the radio crackled. "This is Speed," he said breathlessly. "I've skidded off the course at Skull Chasm! My brakes have failed completely!"

"We have to get to Skull Chasm," Trixie said urgently. "We have to help Speed!"

Trixie flew the helicopter over the mountains and canyons, and the group scanned the ground below for any sign of the Mach 5.

"Look!" Sprite shouted, pointing to a spot below. "There's the Mach 5!"

Sure enough, there was Speed. He was

careening backward, down the slope. As he pressed the A button on his steering wheel, powerful jacks boosted out, acting as additional brakes. Finally, the Mach 5 slowed down and stopped.

Speed wiped his brow. "Whew!" he exclaimed. That had been some ride!

But just as Speed thought he was safe, the ground beneath the Mach 5 gave way and the car flew farther down the chasm.

Desperately, Speed tried to gain control of the car.

"Speed!" Trixie called over the radio.

The Mach 5 continued to race backward down the mountain.

Sparky took control of the radio. "Speed! Jump out!" he cried.

"I can't!" Speed shouted back.

"Jump, Speed!" Sparky urged once more. But he knew that Speed would never leave the Mach 5. If he were to jump out, the Mach 5 would crash and be destroyed.

Thinking quickly, Sparky stood up and picked up some rope. "I'll try to grab the car," he said, swinging the rope over his head like a lasso.

Carefully, Sparky anchored one end of the rope inside the helicopter, and then leaned out the door.

As the Mach 5 continued its slide down the mountainside, Sparky swung the lasso. Incredibly, it caught the front end of the Mach 5 right underneath its tires. Instantly, the car was jerked into the air.

"Agh!" Speed cried as he was flung from the driver's seat.

The empty Mach 5 hung from the rope. "Speed! Where are you?" Sparky cried.

"Ugh, ugh!" was all Speed could muster as he hung by one hand from the car's rear fender. Speed's stomach dropped as he looked down to the chasm's bottom below him and his car above him.

Uttering loud grunts and groans, Speed finally managed to climb back toward the driver's seat.

"Pull it now!" Sparky called to Trixie who was operating the rope winch from her seat.

Slowly and steadily, the helicopter pulled the Mach 5 by the rope up the steep mountainside.

Finally, Speed was pulled to safety. Trixie landed the helicopter, and the group ran out to greet their friend.

"Speed!" Sparky called to his friend, who was lying on the hood of the car with his eyes closed.

"Are you all right?" a worried Trixie asked.

Slowly, Speed's eyes began to open.

Sparky was relieved to see that Speed was okay. "That was a very close call," he said.

Speed put out his hand to Sparky. "I'm sorry for what I said," Speed told him.

Taking Speed's hand, Sparky said, "I'm sorry. I shouldn't have left when you needed me."

"Well, let's forget about it, okay?" Speed said with a grin.

"Okay," Sparky agreed.

Trixie was glad the friends had made up. But then she reminded them that they needed to fix the Mach 5's brakes so Speed could get back in the race.

"I'll help them," Speed said, but then he grunted in pain and grabbed his arm. He had been hurt when the car fell from the mountainside.

"Just take it easy, Speed," Sparky said, rolling under the car. "Fixing the Mach 5 is my job."

"He's right," Trixie said, grabbing Speed by the hands. "And you'd best use the time for resting up, Speed. You have a lot more racing to do, so go over there and sit down." She pushed him toward the helicopter.

"But, Trixie, I'll be all right," Speed protested.

"Do as I say!" Trixie commanded. "Rest!"

When Spritle saw Trixie leading Speed toward the helicopter, he shook his head. "We can't make Speed do anything he doesn't want to. Only Trixie knows how to handle him. But I don't want her giving him my snack! Come on, Chim Chim," he said, pulling the chimp over to the helicopter.

Once inside the helicopter, Trixie told Speed that she heard over the radio that the other racers were taking a break. She offered Speed some lunch. But when she reached for the lunch basket, it was gone!

Trixie knew exactly who the culprit was. "Put

that back!" she called to Spritle.

Spritle appeared at the helicopter's door, an innocent look on his face. "It's my lunch, Speed," he began. "But I'll be glad to do without it. Here, take it."

"You're fibbing, Spritle," an annoyed Trixie said. "You've already had your snack. Go away!"

Spritle didn't know what to say. With a disappointed look on his face, he and Chim Chim walked away.

"Hey, somebody! Please bring me some grease!" Sparky called from under the car.

"Okay!" Spritle said, perking up. Throwing Trixie a mean look, he ran over to a box and started rifling through it.

"Here you are!" Spritle cried triumphantly, holding up a can.

Sparky shook his head. "That's oil. Give me some grease!"

"Is this what you want?" Trixie piped up, holding another can.

"Yes," Sparky said. "Thanks very much, Trixie!"

"Too many mechanics might spoil a car," Spritle said, pointing his finger at Trixie. "Let me help him!"

"Get out of the way!" Trixie said, giving Spritle a push.

Spritle fell down, but jumped up as soon as he hit the ground. *"Grrr!"* he growled, his hands poised like a boxer. "You always think I'm in the way! Nobody talks to me like that! Not even you, Trixie! Bring it on! Come on!"

Spritle threw a little jab at Trixie, but she was

too fast for him. Quickly, she ran away from Spritle and into Speed's arms.

Spritle continued to box and weave. "Nobody says I'm in the way! I'll show her!"

"Spritle, you better stop it," Speed warned.

Spritle looked up and saw that his brother was hugging Trixie. "Hey! What's going on? What's up?" he wanted to know.

Speed and Trixie turned red. Then Speed picked up Trixie and carried her toward the helicopter.

"Speed! Put me down! What are you going to do?" Trixie cried.

Speed threw Trixie onto a seat in the helicopter. "Now you take a rest!"

Spritle walked up to Trixie with a smug look on his face. "You see, Trixie, I'm not the one in the way—you are!"

But Speed wasn't going to stand for Spritle talking to his girlfriend that way. He scooped up Spritle. "Okay, you're next!"

"What did I do wrong?" Spritle cried. "Put me down!"

"There you are!" Speed said, tossing Spritle into the helicopter.

With Trixie and Spritle out of the way, Speed walked over to help Sparky with the car. Speed grabbed a wrench and slid under the Mach 5.

"Well, now the brakes are in perfect working order," Sparky said a while later. "How about you, Speed? You haven't rested a minute. You've been on the go since we got here and you must be pretty tired by now."

Speed put down his wrench and wiped the grease from his hands on his pants. "At least the work's all done now," he said.

Sparky stuck out his hand toward Speed. "Let's let bygones be bygones, and no matter how much we fight, let's always be pals."

Speed smiled and shook Sparky's hand.

"And we should never argue over you racing in the Mach 5," Sparky added.

"We won't," Speed said, patting the car on the door. "The Mach 5 means too much to us. After all, our lives are wrapped up in this car."

Just then, Spritle walked over. "I'm sorry for being such a bad boy," he said sheepishly.

"Spritle, you were supposed to be taking a rest. Why aren't you?" Speed asked.

Spritle held up a little doll with a striped shirt, straw hat, and bucktoothed smile. "I'll let you have my friend for good luck," he told his brother.

"But, Spritle, isn't this supposed to be your good luck charm?" Speed asked.

Spritle nodded. "But I want you to have it, Speed. Just make a wish on it and it might come true. Wish for winning the race!"

Speed took the doll. "All right. I'd like to win."

"Now, maybe you will!" Spritle said excitedly.

Speed was glad everyone had made up. Now he had to apologize to Trixie. He went inside the helicopter, but Trixie was fast asleep. Speed yawned and looked up at the dark blue sky. The sun was setting and deep pink clouds streaked the sky. *Maybe it isn't such a bad idea to get some rest,* Speed thought. He found a blanket and spread it on the ground outside. As he laid his weary body on the ground, he stared up at the starry sky. And in a minute, he was fast asleep.

The next morning, Speed woke with a start. "I've been sleeping too long," he said to himself. "I better hurry or I'll be late getting back into the race."

As he put on his helmet, a streak of lightning crossed the sky. A chill went through Speed's body, as the wind kicked up. *The storm's coming,* he thought.

Quickly, Speed jumped into the Mach 5 and gunned the engine.

Startled by the noise, Sparky woke up. "What's happening?" he asked groggily.

"I'm on my way, Sparky," Speed told his friend. "Say good-bye to everyone."

"Be careful!" Sparky called as the car raced away. "And good luck!"

Speed drove down the road, flashes of lightning streaking across the sky. Each time the thunder cracked, sheets of rain poured down from the sky. For a few miles, the Mach 5 was the only car on the road. Speed knew that he had to drive carefully in this weather, but at the same time, he had to win the race.

As Speed strained his eyes to see the road up ahead, he spotted a group of cars. It was the Car Acrobatic Team, and it looked as if they had stopped. Speed pressed on the brake and slowed the car down.

He drove up beside Snake Oiler. "What's going on?" Speed asked.

Snake looked at Speed in surprise. "I was sure you wouldn't make it," he said shaking his head. "But, look!" He pointed to a road crossing to the

other side. The road had two large breaks in it,
which meant the drivers would have to jump the
gaps in order to continue on the course.

"With the heavy rain, parts of the course have
been completely washed away," Snake explained.
"It's going to be tough."

"Maybe we could take another way," Speed
reasoned.

Snake shook his head. "There is no other way.
And when we try to get through, there'll be more
landslides. Besides, our tires won't take hold in that
wet ground. We've decided to draw lots to see
which one of us goes first. It'll be more dangerous
for each one following."

Speed considered what Snake said. He was right. It would be dangerous for the first car to attempt the jump. But the first car would loosen rocks and kick up mud, making it harder for the cars that followed.

"It is a fair way to do it," Speed told Snake.

Snake turned to face the other racers. "Everyone who wants to draw for being first, step forward."

No one moved.

"What's the matter with you guys?" Snake Oiler asked with an exasperated look on his face. "Are you race car drivers or chickens?"

Slowly, a few drivers stepped forward.

Snake turned back to Speed. "All right, now, come on. What about you, Speed?"

"I'll draw," Speed agreed.

Snake smiled. "Good. Well, finally, we know who the brave men are and who the chickens are!"

Just then, an avalanche of boulders tumbled down the mountainside. Seeing this, several drivers stepped back. They did not want to risk their lives on the jump.

"Wait a minute!" a voice called out.

Speed spun around. "It's Racer X!"

"I'm staying in the race, and I want to join the drawing to see who the first driver will be," Racer X announced.

Snake made a small bow. "Be my guest," he said. "But it won't make any difference because I'm going to be the only one to get through!"

Racer X turned to Speed and said, "I'm glad you're safe, Speed. But you have only one life, so you better be careful."

Speed considered Racer X's words. By being careful, did Racer X mean he shouldn't race? Speed shook his head. He was going for it!

"Now let's get it over with. Let's draw lots. I have six matches." Snake held them out for all to see. "Each one has marks on it," he continued. "One mark means that driver will go first. The other positions will be according to the marks on the matches."

The first driver stepped up to draw. With his hand shaking, he pulled a match from the bundle.

"It's just got one notch on it," the driver cried out, looking at the match. "That means I go first! I go first! Wahoo!"

"You draw next, Tiger." Nervously, Tiger picked a match.

"I'm in third place," he announced.

The next driver up drew second.

Only three drivers were left—Speed, Racer X, and Snake.

"I'll draw last," Racer X offered. "You go

ahead and draw, Speed."

Speed reached for a match. "Oh! Six notches!" Speed cried. "I drew last position!"

Snake laughed. Then he offered the matches to Racer X, who drew fifth position.

"It's all settled then, isn't it?" Snake said. "I get the fourth position, don't I?" He turned to the other drivers. "Start the engines!"

The first car took off down the road. It sprung across the gap and flew into the air. But it missed the landing on the other side and tumbled into the chasm below.

The second car also bounced over the gap and plummeted down.

"Okay, Tiger," Snake said. "It's up to you to make it now!"

Tiger took off down the muddy road and flew smoothly over the chasm. But at the last second, he ended up short of the landing and, like the cars before him, crashed down below.

Upon seeing this third crash, Racer X shook

his head. "The drivers on the Car Acrobatic Team are supposed to be better than that," he said.

"They are!" Snake countered. "And I'll show you! Just watch. I'm going to make that jump safely and prove to you what a fabulous driver I am."

Snake hopped into his car and took off down the now very muddy road. His car wings jutted out and he jumped over the first gap, touching down on the ground. Then he flew over the second gap. The car landed with a thud, but then slipped off the cliff. As the car fell, large pieces of the road broke away and slid down the mountain. The other racers hung their heads as the sound of

Snake's car crashing into the chasm below echoed in their ears.

Racer X turned to face Speed. "Every time a driver tries to make it, some more of the earth caves in, and it's going to get even worse when we try to make the jump. But as a professional racer, I've got to meet the challenge."

Racer X jumped into his car. "If you're smart, you'll give up the race," he called to Speed. "But if you don't, good luck!"

And with that, he took off. Speed watched Racer X land jump after jump until he disappeared. But Racer X had caused more earth to break away. But did Racer X make it to safety? The only way Speed could find out was to attempt the jumps himself.

Speed took a deep breath. The wind was howling and the rain was coming down even harder than before. Without a moment's more hesitation, he jumped into the Mach 5 and secured his seat belt.

"Here I go!" Speed called out to the other racers.

Just as he was about to pull away, three of his competitors ran up to his car.

"Don't go, kid!" one of the racers pleaded. "There's no disgrace if you turn back now!"

"That's right, Speed!" another racer put in. "You're just going to throw yourself down into that chasm if you jump now."

Speed didn't know what to do. He looked at the road on the other side of the gap. A lot of rock was gone, making the landing even more difficult than before.

As he sat there, considering his options, he heard Racer X's voice in his head: *As a professional racer, I've got to meet the challenge.*

And that's just what Speed was, too—a professional.

Speed flipped down his visor and grabbed on to Spritle's good luck charm. He was about to attempt the most dangerous jumps of his life!

While Speed was getting ready to take the dangerous jumps, Trixie, Sparky, Spritle, and Chim Chim were inside an alpine house, taking cover from the storm.

"That's the worst storm I've ever seen!" Sparky said, looking out the window. The rain was pelting the house, and the wind was howling. Sparky blinked as lightning lit up the sky, illuminating the snowcapped mountains.

"It's awful!" Trixie agreed, covering her ears as a loud clap of thunder burst.

Suddenly, the door swung open and a man in a trench coat ran inside the house. He shook the excess water off his clothing and stamped his feet on the wooden floor.

As everyone stared at the man, he announced, "According to this bulletin, more than a dozen cars, including members of the Car Acrobatic Team and the Mach 5, have stopped near Yawning Chasm Pass. The course has been deemed too dangerous."

Sparky and Trixie looked at each other in alarm.

"The Racing Committee is considering changing the course to a less dangerous area before the cars and drivers are completely wiped out!" the man continued.

"Oh! I hope Speed will be all right," Trixie said, sounding concerned.

"I hope he won't try to go ahead," Sparky added.

Spritle stepped up in front of Trixie and Sparky, with his arms crossed. "I'm not worried. He took my good luck charm along with him." He patted Chim Chim on the head. "It'll be just as lucky for Speed as it has been for me. Right, Chim Chim?"

Chim Chim looked back at Spritle with worried eyes. It was clear that Chim Chim did not believe what Spritle was saying.

Spritle took one look at the expression on his pet chimp's face and grabbed Sparky's arm. "Please say he'll be all right," he said, sobbing.

Trixie put her arm around Spritle, trying her best to comfort him. But it was hard, especially since she had a feeling that something had gone terribly wrong . . .

Speed looked at Spritle's good luck charm swinging from his rearview mirror. Grabbing the doll, Speed remembered Spritle's words about the doll bringing Speed plenty of good luck.

"I'm going to need it, Spritle," Speed said out loud.

Speed turned on the ignition, put the clutch in place, stepped on the pedal, and took off. By now, the rain was coming down even harder, making the road extremely muddy. Speed had to concentrate especially hard in order to control the car.

The Mach 5 slipped and slid as it raced toward

the first jump. Speed pressed the A button and the Mach 5 launched into the air.

Next, Speed pressed a new button that Pops had installed on the dashboard. *Zute!* From under each door, small wings popped out, just as planned. The Mach 5 soared through the air, gracefully landing on the first platform. *Phew!* Speed thought as he touched down. But he only had a moment to relax. He needed to make a second jump.

The Mach 5 took off again. The car leaped, but this time only the front wheels landed on the road on the other side. Speed tried to maneuver

the car forward, but it was no use. The back wheels wouldn't catch. The Mach 5 began to slide backward off the cliff! Down, down the mountainside the Mach 5 flew, Spritle's lucky doll spinning in circles.

Speed had lost complete control of the car! Tumbling down the side of the mountain at full speed, Speed saw a small avalanche of rocks following him.

"Aaaah!" Speed screamed, closing his eyes.

As he plummeted down the hill, he thought about all the warnings he had been given. Perhaps everyone was right. Maybe the ice and treacherous mountain course had been too dangerous for him.

Suddenly, the Mach 5 slammed into something hard.

And Speed's world went dark.

Back at the alpine house, two race car drivers burst through the door. They were dripping with rain and were white as ghosts. Their breath came out in deep gasps.

"Aren't you supposed to be in the race?" Sparky asked the men. But as soon as Sparky spoke the words, he knew that these men were in no condition to race—they looked as if they were about to collapse on the floor!

One of the drivers dropped his head to catch his breath. "We barely made it back from Yawning Chasm Pass."

"The road's impassable!" the second driver added.

Sparky looked worried. "Do you know what happened to some of the other drivers in the race?" he asked.

The first driver shook his head. "Most of them will never come back," he answered.

Upon hearing that, Trixie cried out in alarm.

"They tried to make it from one cliff to the other and failed," one of the men said, clutching his chest in pain.

"Are you saying they didn't make it?" Sparky asked in alarm. "Were their cars wrecked?"

The driver walked over to the couch to sit down. "There was nothing left of them, including the cars of the Car Acrobatic Team." He shook his head, as if trying to erase a bad memory.

"They were stupid to try to go ahead when

everybody could see that they wouldn't be able to make it," the second driver continued.

Tears began to fall from Spritle's eyes. "Poor Speed," he said. Chim Chim stroked Spritle's arm to try to comfort him.

Suddenly, Trixie snapped into action. "All right, Sparky!" she called. "Come on!"

"Where?" Sparky asked, confused.

"Speed might need help," Trixie told him.

"I want to try to help him, too!" Spritle said, wiping his eyes.

When the others in the room heard this, they tried to warn the group not to go out in the storm.

It was too dangerous. They urged them to stay put until the storm blew over.

But Trixie wasn't going to listen. "Don't worry," she said. "We'll be all right."

"You can't leave now. As soon as the weather's calmed down we'll send out a search party to look for him," one of the men in the house said.

Trixie was determined. "I'm sorry, but by then it might be too late. I'm going now."

"No, you'll never get through," the man insisted, grabbing hold of Trixie's arm. "You better wait."

"I've got to try and help Speed Racer," Trixie said. "Now, let go of my arm!" Trixie tried to free herself from the man's grasp, but no matter how hard she tried, she couldn't break away. Suddenly, Chim Chim jumped on the man's arm and sunk his big teeth into it. With a loud scream, the man let go. As soon as she was free, Trixie made a run for it, with Sparky at her heels.

"Come back here!" the man shouted. As he

tried to run after them, Spritle tackled him to the ground.

With the man down, Spritle and Chim Chim followed Sparky and Trixie to a Jeep that was parked outside. They jumped inside and took off heading for Trixie's helicopter. As they drove through the torrential rain, they could hear the man yelling, "You'll be sorry!"

But Trixie knew that the only thing she'd be sorry about was if she didn't try to help Speed.

The Jeep raced along a mountain road, through the heavy rain and whipping wind.

"I hope we find him," Trixie said.

Finally, the storm passed. The clouds parted, and the sky brightened. But things weren't looking so bright at the bottom of Yawning Chasm Pass. Race cars—or what was left of them—littered the ground. Smoke rose from the wreckage, and moans could be heard from the injured drivers.

Speed Racer lay among the ruins, his eyes shut, not moving a muscle. As the sun blazed in the sky, Speed began to wake up.

He rolled over, stood up, and turned his face toward the sky. "Oh! My eyes, my eyes!" he cried, falling back on the ground. "I can't see."

Desperately, he crawled along the road feeling for tire tracks. He came across something soft. "It's Spritle's good luck charm!"

Speed was glad to find the doll, but what he really needed to find was the Mach 5. Blindly, he wandered around, clutching the doll in one hand and holding out the other as a guide.

Thump! Speed tripped over something that felt like a car part and fell to the ground. "I hope the Mach 5 hasn't been damaged. I'll find a way to go on with the race even though I can't see. I've got to beat the Car Acrobatic Team."

He stood up again. Holding his arms straight out in front of him, he began to walk.

"Where is it? Where's the Mach 5?" he called in frustration.

Slam! "Who's there?" Speed called out, hearing the sound of a car door.

"It's me, Snake Oiler. You're still alive, Speed?"

Speed nodded. "And I'm surprised that after that crash you are."

"What's your story, Speed?" Snake asked. "Don't tell me the Mach 5 isn't running anymore."

Speed whipped his head around, but he still could not see a thing. "Where is the car?"

Snake put his hands on his knees and started to laugh. "You can't see? Well, isn't that just too bad," he said sarcastically.

Speed had nothing to say.

"Well, it looks as if I'm gonna win the Alpine Race," Snake announced. "You better wait here until somebody rescues you. I'm glad to say your racing days are over for good, Speed! I guess that proves I'm a much better driver than you, Speed. I'm on my way to victory!"

And with that, Snake jumped in his car and raced away, forcing a cloud of dust into Speed's eyes. Speed fell to the ground in pain. As he rolled around, desperately trying to clean his eyes, Speed smelled something. It was the oil of the Mach 5's engine!

"I've found it!" Speed cried as his finger touched the body of the Mach 5.

He opened the door and stepped in. After fumbling around for a minute, Speed managed to find the ignition and turn the key. Then he pulled the clutch and stopped.

"I guess the Mach 5 can still run," Speed said. "But how am I going to drive without seeing the road?"

For Speed Racer, the Alpine Race had just become even more dangerous!

Speed held his breath and prepared to floor the accelerator. He had to get back into the race—and fast! Just then, he heard the sound of another car engine.

"I recognize the sound of that car," Speed said to himself. "It can only belong to Racer X and that must mean he survived the jump. Well, so have I—here it goes!"

Speed took off. He grasped the steering wheel, trying hard to visualize the road. Days before the race, he had pored over maps, studying the course very carefully. Now, he tried to imagine all the twists, turns, and bumps he had reviewed.

"Watch out!" Speed called to himself as he felt some rocks hit the side of the Mach 5. With all the concentration he could muster, Speed guided the Mach 5 along the treacherous road.

Racer X glanced in his rearview mirror. Even though he was still racing, he wanted to keep an eye on Speed. Racer X was worried about Speed, and he wanted to make sure nothing else happened to him. "Keep at it, Speed," he said to himself. "You've got a chance to make it—if you're lucky!"

Speed continued to drive blindly. Each time he made it over a rough patch, or hit a rock, he breathed a sigh of relief. Suddenly, Speed felt the Mach 5's tires begin to spin. He was stuck in the mud! Thinking quickly, he felt around for the B button on his steering wheel. He jammed on the button, but nothing happened! Again and again, he pressed the button, but still—nothing.

"I'm stuck!" Speed cried. "The grip tires seem to be broken," he reasoned.

No sooner did he figure that out, than the Mach 5 begin to slide backward. Desperately, Speed tried to gain traction. But it was no use; the Mach 5 was slowly slipping. If Speed didn't gain control of the car soon, he'd be history!

Seeing the danger Speed was in, Racer X pulled over to the side of the road. *Easy, Speed. Ease it out gently,* Racer X coached silently.

Slowly, the Mach 5 inched forward.

Come on, Speed, Racer X thought to himself. *You can't give up now.* Racer X wanted to help Speed, but he knew he had a race to run. And for now, Speed was safe. So he pulled back on the road and sped off. As he drove, a pang of guilt hit him. Hazarding a glance back at Speed, he thought, *I can't leave him there like that—but what choice do I have? What can I . . .*

"Whoa!" Racer X called out. He was heading straight for a rock embankment! Thinking fast, Racer X leaped out of his car. *Bam!* The car crashed into the rock, exploding into a fiery wreck.

"That was a bad crash," Speed said, hearing the explosion. "I heard Racer X take off before me. Maybe that's him. And if it was, I hope he hasn't been hurt." Now Speed was more determined than ever to get his car out of the mud. Not only did he have the race to complete, but Racer X needed his help!

Finally, the Mach 5 was free. Speed sped in the direction from which he heard the crash. When he

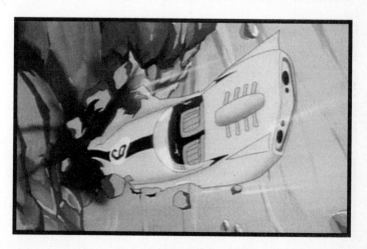

thought he had reached the spot, Speed pulled over and got out of his car. "Racer X! Racer X! Where are you?" Speed called out, feeling his way around the rocks.

Racer X was lying facedown on the ground. Pieces of his former car littered the ground. "Over here, Speed," he said weakly.

"I'm coming," Speed said, walking toward the sound of his voice.

"Uh!" Speed cried out, tripping over a rock.

Racer X, hearing Speed struggling, silently thanked him for coming to his aid. *Speed, you're a brave young man. I'm proud to have you for a brother.*

"Where are you, Racer X? I can't find you!" Speed said, dropping to his knees. Speed groped around on the ground and soon came upon Racer X.

"Are you hurt badly?" Speed asked gently.

"I think my legs are broken, Speed," Racer X said with a groan.

"Well, hang on to me," Speed told him. "I'll try to get you into the Mach 5."

"You need to take care of yourself," Racer X said. "What about your eyes?"

Speed shook his head. "If I don't help you, then neither one of us will be able to win the race."

Racer X sighed. "That's true. Right now Snake Oiler is the only one in the Car Acrobatic Team who's continuing in the race."

"Snake Oiler?" Speed said. "Well, I want to beat him more than anything in the world."

Racer X considered the situation for a moment.

Then he said, "Speed, your car's the only other one that hasn't been damaged. But you can't see and I can't even walk. But, I have an idea that just might work." He put his hand on Speed's shoulder.

Speed was curious. "What is it?"

"You be my legs and at the same time I'll be your eyes," Racer X declared.

"You and I will be a team!" Speed said with a smile.

"Yes, maybe we can overtake Snake and win," Racer X said excitedly. "Come on!"

Racer X slung his arm across Speed's shoulders as Speed guided him to the Mach 5. "I think we have a chance to win!" Speed said to himself as they walked. "A real good chance!"

Speed placed Racer X in the passenger seat, then quickly moved over to the driver's side.

With Racer X as his eyes, Speed raced down the road. "Now ten degrees right," Racer X instructed. "Get ready. Here comes another turn to the right. Fifteen degrees to the right."

As Racer X continued to give instructions, a light on the Mach 5's panel flashed and beeped. With one hand, Speed felt around and picked up the microphone.

"Speed? Speed?" Trixie's voice came over the radio.

"Go ahead, Trixie," Speed said.

"We spotted you from our helicopter," Trixie explained. "Are you all right?"

Speed didn't know what to say. He didn't want to worry Trixie, but he didn't want to lie to her either. "I . . . it's my eyes," he began.

"What's the matter with your eyes?" Trixie asked, alarmed.

Speed tried to reassure her. "I'm perfectly all right. Don't worry—nothing's wrong with them."

But Trixie saw right through Speed. "I think you're fibbing to me," she said.

"Make a left," Racer X cut in.

"Who's that riding with you, Speed?" Trixie wanted to know.

"It's Racer X," Speed explained. "He hurt his legs in a crash."

Sprite grabbed the microphone from Trixie. "Hi, Speed! I'm up here, too!"

Then Sparky grabbed the microphone from Sprite. "Me too," he added.

And Chim Chim, not wanted to be left out, let out a scream.

Upon hearing all his friends' voices, Speed smiled. It felt good to have their support. "Now all I have to do is to beat Snake Oiler," Speed told his friends. "I might be able to catch up with him in the next few minutes. I'll meet you at the finish line, Trixie. Okay?"

Trixie felt proud of Speed. He never gave up, no matter how trying the situation. "I'll be waiting for you, Speed," she said. "Good luck!"

"Faster!" Racer X cut in.

Speed put the microphone back and slammed on the gas.

With Racer X's eyes and Speed's driving skills, the Mach 5 easily sped through all the twists and turns of the road.

"The final checkpoint is two hundred and fifty yards up ahead," Racer X announced. "Put your brakes on."

As the car screeched to a halt, two servicemen ran up to them.

"I'm glad to see you're both safe," one of the men said. "Now why don't you both take a break?"

Speed shook his head. "I don't want one."

"But, Speed, you need a rest," Racer X urged.

"Have you seen the Car Acrobatic Team's car?" Speed asked the men.

One of the men nodded. "The car passed by this checkpoint within the hour," he said.

"Thanks," Speed said, revving the engine. "Hang on!" he warned Racer X. He waved good-bye to the servicemen and was off.

"I won't rest until Snake's been beaten," Speed declared.

"Well, then, you'll have to hurry!" Racer X said.

Speed drove faster and faster, a steady stream of sweat running down his face.

"Faster!" Racer X yelled.

The Mach 5 whipped around tight corners, its tires spinning furiously. The car was clocking over 200 miles per hour!

"I see him!" Racer X shouted. "It's Snake Oiler! He's just ahead. At last, Speed, we've caught up to him!"

From his side-view mirror, Snake spotted

Speed gaining on him. But he wasn't about to let Speed catch up. He hit the gas, widening the gap between his car and the Mach 5. As Snake drove, he saw a wooden bridge just up ahead. Snake Oiler sized up the situation. A few boards were missing from the bridge. There was no way the bridge could handle both cars crossing.

Snake Oiler sped across the bridge, more boards falling in his wake. The bridge was practically destroyed!

"Go ahead, Speed," Snake said with a sneer. "It's your turn to try to get over that bridge without crashing down to those rocks on the bottom."

As the Mach 5 neared the bridge, Racer X became alarmed. "Speed, there's a broken bridge

up ahead. You better use your brakes!"

But Speed knew that Snake Oiler had made it over the bridge. And if Snake could do it, so could Speed. He pressed on.

"Stop, Speed!" Racer X said. "That bridge is falling apart. You better use the brakes before it's too late and we smash up!"

Speed shook his head. "I'm not giving up now!" he said. "Tell me when we get to the broken bridge. I'm going to cross it."

Racer X was becoming upset. "But the Car Acrobatic Team cars have special equipment for flying. The Mach 5 can't do it. Use the brake!"

"I'm going for it!" Speed shot back, ignoring Racer X's warning.

Racer X didn't know what to do. He knew that Speed wanted to win the race, but this was just too dangerous. He had to stop. "Speed, we can't make it! Jam on the brakes! Quick!"

Speed refused to listen. He was determined to win—no matter what the cost.

Determined to jump over the chasm, Speed pressed the A button on the Mach 5's steering wheel. Instantly, superpowered jacks shot out from the bottom of the car. As the Mach 5 bounced high into the air, Speed activated the wings and the car flew over the bridge. In a flash, it landed on the other side. It was close, but they had just made it!

Speed wiped the sweat from his brow as more boards broke loose from the bridge. A couple of

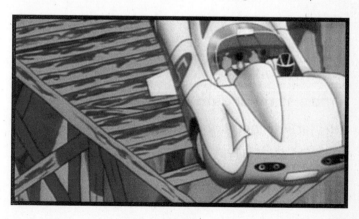

seconds later, the entire bridge crashed onto the rocks below.

"You made it!" Racer X exclaimed, looking back at the spot where the bridge once was. "I didn't think you could have done that even with your eyes open!"

"I didn't have a choice," Speed told him. "I had to make it. Now I've got to win!"

Meanwhile, at the stadium, the crowd was anxiously awaiting the arrival of the drivers. The bleachers were jam-packed with spectators who had their eyes glued on the finish line.

"The Alpine Race is almost over," the announcer told the crowd. "And because of the terrible storm and the dangerous course, out of the starting lineup of eighty-six cars, only two cars are still in the race."

A murmur arose from the crowd. They could

not believe that there were only two cars left!

The announcer continued, "One of them is car number twelve, driven by Snake Oiler of the Car Acrobatic Team. And the other is the Mach 5, driven by Speed Racer. Ladies and gentlemen, if you look to your left, you can see the remaining members of the Car Acrobatic Team waiting for the end of the race."

The members of the Car Acrobatic Team were all lined up. And in the middle of them stood the fearsome-looking, skull-faced Captain Terror.

"Captain Terror!" one of the team members called.

"Yes!" Captain Terror snapped back angrily.

"I just got a report that Snake is in the lead," the driver reported.

Another team member spoke up. "Snake's my brother, and he's going to bring a glorious victory to the Car Acrobatic Team."

"We will be famous as the greatest racing team in the world," Captain Terror declared. "No one can beat us!" Stretching his arms outward and upward he said, "Hurry, Snake—bring us the Crown of Victory!"

As the crowd anxiously waited at the stadium, Speed and Racer X continued to race at a blinding clip. They were desperately trying to overtake Snake Oiler.

"It's hard to catch up to him," Speed said. "He's liable to win. If only I could see, I'd go faster."

"But, Speed, you mustn't give up," Racer X urged.

"Why not?" Speed asked, feeling a bit defeated. "I don't think I have a chance of beating him."

Racer X tried to boost Speed's spirits. "Speed, you still have a chance to win. I can see something you can't. Oil is leaking from Snake's car."

"Oil?" Speed asked in surprise.

Racer X nodded. "If he keeps on going at his present speed, he's going to blow up."

"He may notice the trouble and stop to fix the leak," Speed countered.

"I don't even think he'll notice it. Snake's paying too much attention to the road in front of him," Racer X said.

"Then he'll be wiped out if his car blows up!" Speed concluded.

"Yes," Racer X agreed. "It might be the end of him. But we're not going to help him. Not if you want to win the race."

But even though Snake Oiler was a tricky competitor, Speed was concerned about him. He didn't think it was right not to warn Snake about the danger he was in.

Meanwhile, Snake zoomed into the stadium for

the final lap. Snake glanced in his side-view mirror and gasped. The Mach 5 was right behind him!

"Huh?!" Snake exclaimed. "The Mach 5 again? And it's gaining on me."

The Mach 5 pulled up to the side of Snake's car. Speed turned to Snake to try to get his attention.

"Snake, be careful," Speed warned. "There's something wrong with your engine! You're leaking oil!"

"I'm not falling for that trick! I'm not gonna stop!" Snake gunned his engine and pulled ahead.

"Snake! I'm not lying!" Speed called out.

"He won't believe you, and you've done your best to warn him," Racer X said.

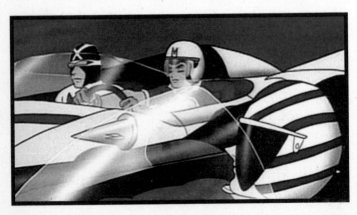

"I know," Speed agreed. "Hang on."

"And now, approaching the finish line is car number twelve, driven by Snake Oiler. It looks like he'll be the winner!" the announcer said.

The crowd cheered.

"Oh, but here comes the Mach 5 with Speed Racer at the wheel," the announcer said excitedly. "Look at them go!"

The crowed cheered even louder.

"Go, Speed! Go!" Spritle called out.

Trixie clasped her hands together. "Go!" she shouted.

"Come on, Speed! You can do it!" Sparky added.

But Snake was sure he was going to take first place. "I'm gonna win! I'm gonna beat Speed Rac—"

Boom! Flames shot out from the rear wheels of Snake's car.

Captain Terror cried out while watching from the sidelines.

Snake screamed as he jumped from the car, just moments before it exploded.

Speed shook his head. "If only he had listened," he said with concern.

But now Speed was the only driver left in the race. He gave the Mach 5 some gas and glided across the finish line.

As soon as the Mach 5 came to a stop, Trixie, Spritle, and Chim Chim dashed out onto the racetrack.

Speed stepped out of the car. He'd won! Even though he still could not see, he could feel and hear the excitement in the stadium. He could picture everyone on their feet, cheering and waving white hankies. As he raised his face toward the sky, bits

of confetti landed on it. Beaming, Speed waved to his fans. Trixie took his arm and guided him to a platform so he could accept his prize.

"You drove a magnificent race, Speed Racer," a judge said. He handed Speed a big trophy and shook his hand.

"You fully deserve to be the winner and champion," the judge continued. Speed felt very proud. He bowed to the judge in thanks.

"Now you better get to the hospital so the doctors can take care of your eyes," the judge added.

Everyone was happy for Speed, except for Captain Terror and the Car Acrobatic Team. Captain Terror walked over to the smoldering remains of car number twelve and picked up Snake Oiler. He was badly hurt, but he was still alive.

"We will never forget this race and our defeat by Speed Racer," Captain Terror said.

Snake slowly turned his head toward Captain Terror. "We'll get revenge," he whispered.

"We shall plan for the day when, once again, we will compete against Speed Racer. And on that day we shall not fail!" Captain Terror said.

Placing Snake Oiler into his car, Captain Terror drove off, with the rest of the Car Acrobatic Team following.

As the Car Acrobatic Team drove off, Trixie, Spritle, and Chim Chim guided Speed toward their car. They were going to take him to the hospital to get his eyes checked. Speed was also anxious to see Pops so he could tell him all about his adventure.

"Have you seen Racer X?" Speed asked Trixie. "I've got to find him to thank him."

"I saw him in the Mach 5 only a few minutes ago," Trixie replied.

"Nobody's in the car now," Spritle said.

Speed was surprised. "There isn't? That means he was able to walk! His legs weren't broken. He just told me that so I'd let him help drive. He deserves this trophy—not me."

"Oh, Speed, all that matters to me is that you finished safely," Trixie said, putting her hand on Speed's shoulders. "Now, let's go to the hospital and get your eyes taken care of."

From a distance, Racer X watched Speed walk away with his friends. "Speed, you could be a great driver, but you could also be a great man," he said to himself. "You value life even more than victory. The world needs more people like you—I'm proud to have you as a brother!"

A year has passed since I last met Captain Terror and the Car Acrobatic Team. I've entered many races since then, but none have been as dangerous as the Alpine course.

I will never forget that grueling race over treacherous mountain trails. And I will never forget the Car Acrobatic Team. Racer X warned me about them. He told me not to race against them. He said that the Car Acrobatic Team would stop at nothing to win. However, his warning did not stop me, and as you know, I went on to win.

After the race, Captain Terror vowed vengeance against me. He swore that one day we would meet again. And when we did, he promised he would beat me.

Yes, we would meet again. But beat me? Well, start your engines—you are about to find out what happened . . .

The sky was streaked with dark clouds, which hung low above the Alps. Down below, a lone figure stepped out from the mist, his cape whipping in the wind.

"It was one year ago that Speed Racer and his Mach 5 defeated us," the man announced to a group of men holding flaming torches.

"Yes, Captain Terror," the men responded. They were the members of the dreaded Car Acrobatic Team.

"We swore that someday we would get our revenge," Captain Terror continued. "That time is almost at hand! We will race against Speed Racer

again, and this time we will not only defeat him, we will destroy him!" Captain Terror let out an evil laugh. The members of the Car Acrobatic Team shuddered.

"We will challenge Speed to a race, which of course he will accept. Then, once again, we, the great Car Acrobatic Team, will be recognized as the greatest racers in the world!"

A streak of lightning crossed the sky, followed by a loud clap of thunder. Rain came down from the sky, extinguishing the torches, and everything turned dark.

That night, Speed Racer had a dream that he was talking to Captain Terror.

"Do you remember when we raced a year ago, Speed?" Captain Terror said. "Think back and remember it well. How could you forget?" The

Captain's image spun in circles in Speed's mind.

"We will race you again, soon, over the same treacherous trails, across the same yawning chasms, over the same brinks of disaster, and we will beat you!" Captain Terror said with a terrifying laugh.

Speed woke up with a start. To his surprise, he found a letter from Captain Terror lying next to his pillow. It was a letter challenging him to a race. Speed's dream had come true! Quickly, Speed changed into his racing gear and hopped into the Mach 5. In a flash, he drove out of the garage and into the blinding storm.

As Speed drove through the night down a lonely highway, he came upon a figure standing in the road with his arms stretched out. Was this person in trouble? Did he need Speed's help? Speed stepped on the gas. As he reached the figure, he slowed down and discovered it was Racer X!

Racer X ran up to the Mach 5. "Speed, a race is not a fight. Don't accept the challenge of the Car Acrobatics."

"How did you find out about the race, Racer X?" Speed wanted to know.

Racer X shook his head. "Never mind. You're a professional racer, and a professional racer doesn't fight, he races! And he doesn't hold private grudge races. Go home and forget about a grudge race against the Car Acrobatic Team."

"I can't," Speed told him. "They'll think I'm afraid to accept their challenge to another race. They'll think I can't beat them again. Now get out of the way!"

"Don't be a fool," Racer X warned.

But Speed didn't listen. He drove off, leaving Racer X in his dust.

Back at the Racer home, Pops Racer was sick in bed. He was surrounded by Trixie, Spritle, and Chim Chim. They were all worried about him.

"What a fine day for me to catch a cold, the day before an important race!" Pops said weakly, trying to prop himself up.

"You've got to stay in bed, Pops," Trixie said, gently pushing him back down on the bed. "You're running a very high fever!"

Pops wiped the sweat from his brow. "I wish my oldest son, Rex, were here. I wonder where he is now. If only he hadn't disobeyed me years ago and entered that race. That was when all the trouble started. He was too young, too inexperienced to compete against the professional race car drivers."

In that race, Rex lost control of his car just before the finish line and crashed into a wall. Rex wasn't hurt, but Pops was shaken up. He forbade Rex to become a professional racer. Pops wanted him to wait until he was older and had more experience behind the wheel.

But Rex refused to listen. "You can't stop me from racing," he told Pops. "Racing's in my blood, and I'm going to continue doing it!"

Pops and Rex continued to argue, but Rex still wouldn't obey. He was determined to race—no matter what. So he ran away from home!

Pops tossed and turned in his bed. His fever climbed higher and higher. "I hope Rex comes home someday," Pops whispered.

At a house in another part of town, a secret meeting was taking place.

"Is everybody here?" a man dressed in white asked. He was carrying a cane, and he tapped his peg leg nervously on the floor as he spoke.

"Yes, Mr. Supremo," answered one of the many men who was sitting at a long table.

"All right, Mr. Magnito," Mr. Supremo said, taking a seat. "Give me the report."

Mr. Magnito cleared his throat and began. "As you know, the international secret police have been smashing our secret branch offices. We've discovered that one man is behind these disasters. Take a look at this," Mr. Magnito said, pointing to a screen.

"The secret agent goes under the name of Racer X," Mr. Magnito explained as slides flashed on the screen. Sure enough, there were pictures of Racer X!

"Some of our best brains and top agents have proven to be no match for Racer X," Mr. Magnito continued. "Time and time again Racer X and his friends have out-tricked and out-fought our agents. We cannot underestimate the threat this man poses to our future."

Mr. Supremo banged his cane on the ground. "I've heard enough! The report is about nothing but failure, failure, failure! What have you people been doing to get rid of Racer X?"

"Everything we can, sir," Mr. Magnito said. "But watch carefully. There's more to our report. Racer X is not the only one who has caused trouble. A great many of our agents have been defeated by another young man."

Mr. Supremo looked surprised. "Who is he?"

"A professional racer," Mr. Magnito responded. "One of the best—his name is Speed Racer. He drives a powerful, specially designed and built car called the Mach 5. Here you see film clips of the great Alpine Race where he competed against the Car Acrobatic Team, among others. In a moment, you will see and learn something fascinating. Watch closely!"

"I'm watching! I'm watching!" Mr. Supremo said impatiently.

Mr. Magnito pointed toward the screen. "And there you are—Speed Racer and Racer X racing side by side!"

Mr. Supremo shrugged his shoulders. "So they competed against each other in the same race. So what?"

Mr. Magnito sighed. "But Mr. Supremo, we've discovered that Racer X is secretly Speed Racer's older brother, Rex Racer, who ran away from home years ago."

"What?!" Mr. Supremo exclaimed in amazement.

"It's true," Mr. Magnito replied. "And not even Speed Racer knows Racer X is his brother!"

"That's astounding! But are you sure it's true?" Mr. Supremo asked.

"Compare their photographs," Mr. Magnito urged. "See the resemblance for yourself."

Mr. Supremo scratched his chin and nodded. "So you have been busy after all. A magnificent job!"

Mr. Magnito breathed a sigh of relief and smiled. "Our next step is to get rid of Racer X forever. This is the Car Acrobatic Team," he said, pointing to another slide. "They plan to race against Speed soon. We're certain that Racer X will also be around. He knows that the Car Acrobatics are out for revenge, and he'll want to protect his younger brother, Speed. That will give us the opportunity we've been looking for. We will find Racer X and destroy him!"

"What about Speed?" Mr. Supremo wanted to know.

"Why worry about him?" Mr. Magnito said with a shrug. "Without Racer X to protect him, he'll be an easy target for the Car Acrobatics. They'll take care of him for us. All we have to do is concentrate on getting Racer X."

"Very clever, Mr. Magnito. You have everything

worked out excellently!" Mr. Supremo said with an evil laugh.

"Now, sir," Mr. Magnito said. "I suggest we put the plan into effect."

◎　　◎　　◎　　◎

After driving all night, Speed Racer found Captain Terror and the Car Acrobatic Team in the middle of a dark road.

"We've been waiting for you, Speed," Captain Terror said. "As you can see, we accepted your letter challenging us to one more race. And this time, you will lose badly!"

"Wait a minute," Speed said. "What do you mean my letter challenging you? I got a letter from you challenging me to one more race!"

Captain Terror looked confused.

"That's why I came," Speed continued. "Regardless of how we both came here, I plan to race against you and win!"

Upon hearing this, Captain Terror was outraged. "No, you won't! We are the greatest racers in the world, and this time we'll prove it!"

"You failed to prove it the last time we met, and you'll fail again," Speed shot back. "I'm warning you! I'm going to win!"

"We'll see," Captain Terror said. "Come on, Speed. Let's go!"

Everyone immediately jumped into their cars and sped down the course. As the rain continued to pour down, the cars sped down the mountain

road, packed tightly together. They raced past waterfalls and over slippery rocks. As the cars approached a steep incline, Speed managed to take the lead. And just as he made it to the top, three of the Car Acrobatic Team cars slipped and crashed into the canyon below.

As Speed paused to survey the fiery crash, one of the Acrobatic drivers passed him and took the lead. Taken off guard, the Mach 5's tires slipped and dangerously teetered on the end of the road.

"He's going over the cliff!" the Car Acrobatic Team driver observed. But no sooner did he utter those words than his own car tumbled off the road and into the water below.

Miraculously, Speed edged his way back on the road and regained the lead.

Meanwhile, from afar, Racer X was driving in his car and trying his best to keep his eye on Speed. But suddenly, his path was blocked. Racer X stopped his car, got out, and came face-to-face with Mr. Magnito and two other thugs.

"We've been waiting for you, Racer X, or should I say Rex Racer, the international secret agent?" Mr. Magnito said, stepping out of his car.

"What's going on?" Racer X shot back.

"We're going to get rid of you forever so you never interfere with us again," Mr. Magnito said.

But before Mr. Magnito and his men could make a move, Racer X jumped back into his car and made a 180 degree turn.

"After him!" Mr. Magnito shouted. A dozen black sedans appeared from behind Mr. Magnito and followed Racer X.

Racer X checked his rearview mirror and made a sharp turn, sending a few of the black cars crashing into the side of the mountain.

A littler farther down the road, Racer X spotted one of the thugs lying injured beside his car.

Seeing that no one was behind him, Racer X stopped his car and jumped out. He wanted some answers. "Why did you try to get rid of me?" Racer X asked, standing over the man. "Who are you and what's the name of your organization? Come on, tell me!"

"Uh, uh," the man stuttered. "I'm with International Spies, Incorporated, and we want to get rid of you and your brother," the man said nervously.

Racer X couldn't believe his ears. "You're trying to get rid of my brother, Speed?"

The man nodded. "We set time bombs in all of the Car Acrobatic Team's cars. Since Speed is racing with them, when the bombs in their cars go off, it'll be the end of them all!"

"I've got to reach Speed before those time bombs in the Car Acrobatic Team's cars go off," Racer X said urgently, hopping back into his car.

By now, the sedans were gaining ground on Racer X. While one of his associates drove, Magnito kept a close eye on Racer X. Suddenly, Racer X swerved off the road, and in an instant was out of sight. Thinking that Racer X had fallen off the side of a cliff, Mr. Magnito was satisfied. He called his boss, Mr. Supremo, to give him the news.

Back at the race, Captain Terror and Speed were flying down a narrow dirt road that hung over a river.

Captain Terror, who was in the lead, glanced into his rearview mirror and cackled. "This road is so narrow that Speed can't possibly pass me and pull into the lead."

Unbeknownst to the drivers, Racer X was still alive. He made his way up a back road and stopped right in front of Captain Terror's car!

"What are you doing?" Captain Terror shouted, slowing his car to a stop. "Can't you see you're in the middle of a race? Get your car out of the way!"

Just then, Speed pulled up behind Captain Terror's car. "Wait a minute—that man's Racer X!"

"You've got to stop the race immediately," Racer X warned them. "There are time bombs planted in every one of your cars."

Captain Terror looked alarmed. "Time bombs? What are you talking about?"

"I found out that the challenging letters you each got were phony," Racer X explained. "You didn't write them to each other. Those letters were sent by the International Spies to trick me into coming here. They want to get rid of me," Racer X explained.

Captain Terror and Speed didn't know what to believe. But they believed that there were bombs in the cars, and they knew they had to work together if they wanted to stop the evil International Spies. So they agreed to call off their race.

"Racer X, you drive with me. Speed will follow in his car, and the rest of the Car Acrobatic Team will follow behind him," Captain Terror declared. "We'll take their time bombs back to them and give them a taste of their own medicine."

Racer X directed them to the spies' headquarters. "Faster! You've got to go faster!" Racer X shouted as Captain Terror drove. "We probably don't have much time left before the bombs go off!"

"Look! There's their hideout!" Racer X said, pointing to a building on top of a hill.

"As soon as we surround the hideout, we'll get away from the cars," Captain Terror said. The cars split formation to fully encircle the building. As soon as the building was completely surrounded by the team's cars, Captain Terror gave the order to his men: "Abandon you cars—run for your lives!" As Speed pulled the Mach 5 to safety, the rest of the men ran for cover.

Inside the building, Mr. Supremo heard a noise. "What was that? Magnito, didn't you hear something just now?"

"It's probably the wind howling through those mountains," Mr. Magnito replied.

As Mr. Supremo started to speak again, a huge explosion went off outside. Car parts and metal shot off in all directions. Moments later, the hideout caught fire.

From the side of a cliff, Speed, Racer X, and Captain Terror stood together, looking at the destruction. They knew that the International

Spies would never recover from this.

"Racer X, how can we thank you?" Captain Terror asked. "If it hadn't been for you, our race with Speed would have ended in disaster."

Just then, a helicopter circled overhead. It was Trixie and the rest of the gang!

"Well, Speed," Racer X observed, "it looks as if your racing team has flown here to pick you up." Then, turning to Captain Terror, he said, "Come on. We might as well get out of here."

"All right, Racer X," Captain Terror agreed.

"Speed, we'll meet again," Captain Terror said with an outstretched hand. "And when we do, I wish you luck."

"When you meet again, I'm sure Speed will beat you again," Racer X added.

Captain Terror smiled. "That's what you think."

And with that, the two men walked away.

"Racer X," Speed called after them.

Slowly, Racer X turned around.

"Are you really my brother, Rex Racer?"

Racer X did not know what to say.

Captain Terror was shocked at this news. He walked up to Racer X and peered under his mask. "You are his brother! I can see the resemblance even under that mask."

Racer X nodded. "I am. But even though I am his brother, I can't go home again. I'm giving up being a racer and from now on I'll be a full-time international secret agent." With that, he pulled his mask off and threw it down on the ground.

"Good-bye, Speed," Racer X said. "I'll try to keep my eye on you and be nearby whenever you need help, no matter where you might go."

Just then, the helicopter landed, kicking up a cloud of dust. When the dust cleared, all that was left was Racer X's mask. Racer X and Captain Terror had disappeared.

"What happened to my brother, Rex?" Speed shouted, running in circles. "Rex, Rex—where are you?"

Trixie jumped out of the helicopter and raced over to Speed. "What is it? Did you find Rex at last?"

Speed looked up at the sky. "Rex, wherever you are, I promise to try to be the best racer in the world and to make you proud of me. Good-bye, Rex."